his book belongs to

. . . .

Endpapers by Oska Paul aged 7¼.

For Sharon and Martin, who are always full of good ideas – V.T.
For Ron Heapy – K.P.

OXFORD
UNIVERSITY PRESS

Great Clarendon Street, Oxford OX2 6DP

Oxford University Press is a department of the University of Oxford.
It furthers the University's objective of excellence in research, scholarship,
and education by publishing worldwide in

Oxford New York

Auckland Cape Town Dar es Salaam Hong Kong Karachi
Kuala Lumpur Madrid Melbourne Mexico City Nairobi
New Delhi Shanghai Taipei Toronto

With offices in

Argentina Austria Brazil Chile Czech Republic France Greece
Guatemala Hungary Italy Japan Poland Portugal Singapore
South Korea Switzerland Thailand Turkey Ukraine Vietnam

Oxford is a registered trade mark of Oxford University Press
in the UK and in certain other countries

First published 1999
First published in paperback 1999
Reprinted 2000, 2002
Reissued with new cover 2006
10 9

British Library Cataloguing in Publication Data
Data available

ISBN 978-0-19-272646-9 (paperback)
ISBN 978-0-19-272669-8 (paperback with audio CD)

Printed in Singapore

Paper used in the production of this book is a natural,
recyclable product made from wood grown in sustainable forests.
The manufacturing process conforms to the environmental
regulations of the country of origin.

www.korkypaul.com

Valerie Thomas and Korky Paul

Winnie
Flies Again

OXFORD
UNIVERSITY PRESS

Winnie the Witch always travelled by broomstick.
It was a wonderful way to travel.

Winnie would jump onto her broomstick.
Wilbur would jump onto her shoulder.
And they would zoom up into the sky.

There were no traffic lights.
No traffic jams.

Just the empty sky.

Well, that was how it used to be.
But, just lately, the sky had become
rather crowded.

Last week, Winnie didn't see a helicopter.
Wilbur lost two of his whiskers.

The week before that,
she didn't see a hang glider.

Wilbur's tail was bent.

The week before that, a very tall building suddenly got in her way.

Wilbur lost a clump of fur.

'The sky is too dangerous, Wilbur,' said Winnie.
'We'll have to try something else.'
So she took out her wand, waved it, and shouted,

ABRACADABRA!

Her broomstick turned into a
bicycle. But it was very slow.
Very hard to pedal.

And then a pond got in Winnie's way.
'She should look where she's going,' croaked a frog.

'A bicycle is worse than a broomstick, Wilbur,' said Winnie.
'We'll have to try something else.'
So she took out her wand, waved it, and shouted,

ABRACADABRA!

Her bicycle turned into a skateboard.
The skateboard was fast.
But it was hard to steer.
And impossible to stop.

Winnie was stopped. By an ice-cream seller.
'Can't you see where you're going?' he shouted.

'A skateboard is worse than a bicycle, Wilbur,' said Winnie.
'We'll have to try something else.'
So she took out her wand, waved it, and shouted,

ABRACADABRA!

Her skateboard turned into a horse,
and they trotted slowly down the path.
'This is much better than bicycles
or skateboards,' said Winnie.

But she didn't see . . .

. . . the low branch of a tree.
This time, Winnie didn't say anything.
She was hanging from a branch.

Slowly and carefully,
Winnie climbed down
from the tree.

'I think we'll walk
home, Wilbur,'
said Winnie.

They limped slowly along the road.
It was a very very slow way to travel.

But it was safe.

Until Winnie stepped into a hole
and tumbled deep down under the ground.

YES
WEeRE
OPEN

'I think I need a
cup of tea,' Winnie said.

Winnie climbed out of the tunnel
and went into a shop.

'A cup of tea and a muffin, please,' she said.
'And a saucer of milk for my cat.'

'We don't sell cups of tea or muffins,'
said the shop lady.
'And we don't have saucers of milk.
But I think I can help you.'

And she sold Winnie a pair of spectacles.

Now, Winnie and Wilbur travel everywhere by broomstick.
It's a wonderful way to travel.